For Grandmother,
with love and gratitude.

All rights reserved. Published in the United States by Tricycle Press, an imprint
of Random House Children's Books, a division of Random House, Inc., New York.
randomhouse.com/kids

Tricycle Press and the Tricycle Press colophon are registered trademarks
of Random House, Inc.

First published in 1989 by Beyond Words Publishing

Library of Congress Catalog Card Number: 89-062534

ISBN 978-1-883672-99-7 (Paperback) / ISBN 978-1-58246-002-4 (Hardcover)

Printed in China

17 16 15 14 13 12 11 10
First Paperback Edition

Other Tricycle Press books by Paul Owen Lewis:
 Grasper
 Storm Boy
 Frog Girl
 Davy's Dream
 The Jupiter Stone

You are cordially invited to

P. BEAR'S

NEW YEAR'S PARTY!

(Formal dress required.)

A Counting book by

PAUL OWEN LEWIS

TRICYCLE PRESS
Berkeley

Mr. P.Bear decided to have
sent invitations to his

a New Year's Party, and
best dressed friends.

At one o'clock, New

Year's Eve, a whale arrived...

at two o'clock, a

couple of horses...

at three o'clock, a

few dairy cows...

at four o'clock, a

herd of zebras...

at five o'clock, o

bunch of panda bears…

at six o'clock, a

half-dozen mountain goats...

at seven o'clock,

several snow leopards...

at eight o'clock, a

pack of dalmatian dogs...

at nine o'clock, lots

of skunks...

at ten o'clock, a

flock of geese...

at eleven o'clock, a

crowd of cats . . .

and, just before twelve

midnight, a dozen penguins!